CHRISTMAS MOON

/ / / /

J.R. RAIN

THE VAMPIRE FOR HIRE SERIES

Moon Dance
Vampire Moon
American Vampire
Moon Child
Christmas Moon
Vampire Dawn
Vampire Games
Moon Island
Moon River
Vampire Sun
Moon Dragon
Moon Shadow
Vampire Fire
Midnight Moon
Moon Angel

Published by
Crop Circle Books
212 Third Crater, Moon

Printed in the United States of America.

ISBN-13: 978-1547199938
ISBN-10: 1547199938

Dedication

To H.T. Night, for all his invaluable help.
Merry Christmas, little brother.

1.

I was cleaning house in the dark and watching Judge Judy rip some cheating ex-husband a new one, when my doorbell rang. Enjoying this more than I probably should have, I hurried over to the door and opened it.

My appointment—and potential new client—was right on time. His name was Charlie Anderson, and he was a tall fellow with a short, gray beard, bad teeth, nervous eyes and a peaceful aura. In fact, the aura that surrounded him was so serene that I did a double take.

I showed him to my back office where he took a seat in one of the four client chairs. I moved around my desk and sat in my leather chair, which made rude noises. I might have blushed if I could have.

I picked up my liquid gel pen and opened my pad of paper to a blank page. I said, "You mentioned in your email something about needing help finding something that was lost."

"Stolen, actually."

I clicked open my pen. "And what was that?"

"A safe," he said.

I think I blinked. "A safe?"

"Yes. A safe. It was stolen from me, and I need your help to find it."

He explained. The safe had been handed down through his family for many generations. It had never been opened, and no one knew what was inside. Charlie's father, now deceased, had left the safe to him nearly twenty years ago. Recently, a gang of hoodlums had moved into Charlie's neighborhood, and soon after, some of Charlie's things had gone missing. A gas can, loose change from the ashtray in his car. If he was a betting man—and Charlie assured me he wasn't—he would bet that these punks had stolen his safe.

I made notes. Charlie spoke haltingly, often circling back and repeating what he'd just said. Charlie was a shy man and he wasn't used to being the center of attention. He was even shy about being the center of attention of a smallish woman in her small back office.

"When was the safe stolen?"

"Two days ago."

"Where was it stolen from?"

"My home. A mobile home. A trailer, really."

I nodded. I wasn't sure I knew what the difference was, but kept that to myself. "And where did you keep the safe in your trailer?"

"I kept it behind the furnace."

"Behind?"

"The furnace is non-functional."

"I see."

"If you remove the blower, there's a space to hide stuff."

I nodded, impressed. "Seems like a good hiding spot to me."

"I thought so, too."

"Any chance it could have been stolen a while back, and you only recently noticed?"

He shrugged. In fact, he often shrugged, sometimes for no apparent reason. Shrugging seemed to be a sort of nervous tic for Charlie. He said, "A week ago, maybe."

"Were you alone when you checked the safe?"

"Yes."

I studied my notes...tapping my pen against the pad. My house was quiet, as it should be.

The kids were at school. As they should be. I looked at the time on my computer screen. I had to pick them up in about twenty minutes.

At about this time of the day, my brain is foggy at best. So foggy that sometimes the most obvious question eludes me. I blinked, focused my thoughts, and ignored the nearly overwhelming desire to crawl back into bed...and shut out the world.

At least until the sunset. Then, I was a new woman.

Or a new *something*.

I kept tapping the tip of the pen against the pad of paper until the question finally came to me. Finally, it did. "Why would the thieves know to look behind the furnace? Seems a highly unlikely place for any thief to ever look."

He shrugged.

I said, "Shrugging doesn't help me, Mr. Anderson."

"Well, I don't know why they would look there."

"Fair enough. Did you ever tell anyone about the safe?"

"No."

"Did anyone ever see you, ah, looking at the safe?"

"I live alone. It's just me."

"Any family members know about the

safe?"

"Maybe a few do, but I don't keep in touch with them."

"Do you have any children?"

"Yes."

Bingo. "Where do your kids live?"

"The Philippines, presently. I'm a retired Navy vet. My ex-wife is from the Philippines. The kids stay with her most of the time."

"But some of the time they stay with you?"

"Yes?"

"How long ago has it been since they were last with you?"

"A month ago."

More notes, more thinking. I put the pen aside. I had asked just about everything my dull brain could think of. Besides, I had to start wrapping this up.

"I can help you," I said. "But under one condition."

"What's that?"

"I get half of whatever's in the safe."

"What about the retainer fee?"

"I'll waive the fee."

"And if you don't find the safe?"

"You owe me nothing," I said.

He looked at me for a good twenty seconds before he started nodding. "I've always wondered what the hell was in that thing."

"So, do we have a deal then, Mr. Anderson?"

"We have a deal," he said.

2.

I picked up the kids from school and, as promised, we made a dollar store run. Once there, I gave the kids each a hand basket and told them to have it.

They had at it, tearing through the store like game show contestants. Tammy crammed some packages of red velvet bows in her hand basket and moved onto the jingle bells, shaking them vigorously. I chuckled as I watched little Anthony grab some scented Christmas candles. The candles filled up at least half his hand basket. Now, what did an eight-year-old need with Christmas candles? Nothing. He simply grabbed them because it was the first of the

Christmas items he'd seen. I was fairly certain that he would later regret his choice.

As the kids attacked the many holiday rows, I smiled to myself and strolled casually through the mostly-clean store, trying like hell to ignore the way my legs shook, or the way my skin still burned from the five-second sprint from the minivan to the store.

Sadly, even with the winter-shortened days, we were still about two hours from sunset.

Two hours.

That thought alone almost depressed me.

Since my transmutation seven years ago, I'm supernaturally aware of the location of the sun in the sky. I can be in any building at any time and tell you exactly where the sun is, either above or below the Earth. Even now I could feel it directly above me, angling just over my right shoulder, heading west.

I powered through the shakiness and heaviness, and worked my way down an aisle of discounted hardback novels. I paused and flipped through a historical mystery novel, read a random paragraph, liked it, and dropped it into my own hand basket. For a buck, I'll try anything. Hell, the Kindle app on my iPhone was filled with free ebooks and .99 cent ebooks that I had snagged in a buying frenzy a few days ago. Now, all I needed to do was to find the time to read them. I'm sure the one about the vampire mom—written, of all people, by a guy with a beard—should give me a good laugh.

I continued down the aisle. I didn't often shop at the dollar store, but when I did, I made the most of it. And the kids, I knew, had been waiting all week for this trip.

It was, after all, a Christmas tradition with us. Each year about this time, the kids were given an empty basket and told to fill them with Christmas decorations. At a dollar a pop, no one was going to break the bank, and once home, together we hung or displayed the decorations. Usually with cookies baking in the oven. Of course, this was the first year we were doing it without Danny, but so far, neither of the kids had mentioned the exclusion of their father, and I sure as hell wasn't going to say anything.

Seven months ago, just after a rare disease nearly cost my son his life, I had filed for divorce. Just last month, the divorce had been finalized. I was technically single, although my relationship with Kingsley Fulcrum had taken on legs. Or teeth. We had grown closer and more comfortable with each other, and for that I was grateful to him.

The famed defense attorney—never known for his moral compass, nor morals of any type —had suddenly developed a conscience. Now, he was a little more selective with his defense cases, a little more discerning. He winnowed out the obvious slimeballs. Of late, he seemed to choose his clients with some care.

He did this, I knew, for me.

After all, I had found it nearly impossible to get too close to a man who actively defended murderers and cutthroats, rapists and all-around jerk-offs. He got it. If he wanted me in the picture, he was going to have to change.

And he did.

Yeah, I'm still amazed and a little in shock.

But we were taking things slowly. I had to move slowly. Anything faster, and I would have seriously freaked out. So I only saw the big lug a few times a week, sometimes only once a week. He never stayed over...and only rarely did I stay over at his palatial estate. Half the time, he took me out. The other half, I cooked for him. It took me months before I formally introduced my kids to him. And even then, I only did so as my "friend."

I knew the friend comment hurt him, but he went with it. Anthony, I knew, had never seen a man this big in his life, and Kingsley was immediately the designated jungle gym. I couldn't help but laugh every time Kingsley showed up, especially in his two-thousand-dollar Armani suits, only to watch Anthony climb all over him.

I chuckled at the recent image of Kingsley sighing resignedly as Anthony used the defense attorney's massive bicep as a pull-up bar. To Kingsley's credit, he always let Anthony play, and never once did he mention his clothes. I figured that someday he would wise up and show up in jeans and a tee shirt.

We'll see.

I had just spotted an end-cap stacked with organic soup. Granted, I couldn't eat organic soup, but my kids could. And at a dollar a pop, I eagerly started scooping them up.

As I did so, I sensed someone behind me and paused and turned.

And gasped.

Okay, a small gasp. After all, I wasn't expecting to see such a beautiful man there, leaning casually against a shelf full of cheap spatulas, and smiling warmly at me. His eyes even twinkled, and I couldn't help but notice the soft, silvery aura that surrounded him. Never before had I seen a silver aura, and never an aura so alive and vibrant.

Who the hell was this guy?

I didn't know, but one thing was for sure: I was especially not expecting him to say my name, but that's exactly what he did.

He crossed his arms over his massive chest,

and said, "Hello, Samantha. How are you?"
This time, I definitely gasped.

3.

A peaceful calm radiated from the tall man.

His silver aura shimmered around him like a halo. His warm smile put me immediately at ease. My inner alarm system, too, since it was as silent as could be. He wore a red cashmere turtleneck sweater, very Christmassy looking, with relaxed fit jeans and hiking shoes. His shoes looked new. His fingers, which curled around his biceps, were long and whitish, capped by pinkish, thick nails.

"Do I know you?" I asked.

"Not directly," he said.

"Indirectly?"

"You could say that."

I wracked my brain. Had he been a client? A

high school boyfriend? A friend of a high school boyfriend? Was he the boy I kissed behind the backstop in the fourth grade? Or the boy I kissed at the bus stop? Other than realizing that I showed a predisposition for love triangles at an early age, my mind remained maddeningly blank, although something nagged at me distantly.

"You got me," I said. "How do you know me?"

He continued leaning against the shelf, watching me. "Through my work."

"Your work?"

He nodded. "Yes."

"And what kind of work is that?"

"I'm a...bodyguard of sorts."

Technically, so was I. As a licensed private investigator in the State of California, I could legally work as a bodyguard, too. Granted, at five-foot three inches tall, I couldn't cover much of anyone's body. Still, I bring other...skill sets to the table.

Despite sensing no danger, my guard was up. I instinctively looked over at my kids, who were presently fighting over a huge Styrofoam candy cane, apparently the only one in the store. The candy cane promptly snapped in half like a wish bone. Anthony let out a wail. Tammy gave him her broken piece and slinked away. I would deal with her later. The kids, at least, were fine.

"I'm sorry," I said to him, "but I don't remember you."

"I wouldn't expect you to."

He spoke calmly, assuredly, with no judgment in his voice. If anything, there was a hint of humor. He watched me closely, his blazing eyes almost never leaving me. Whoever he was, I had his full attention. I nearly just wished him a merry Christmas and turned and left, but something made me stick around.

"So, what's your name?" I asked.

"Ishmael."

I almost made a *Moby Dick* joke, but held back. Truth be known, I was a little freaked out that this guy knew me, and I hadn't a clue who he was.

"Where do you know me from, Ishmael? And give it to me straight. No more double speak."

"I'm afraid you wouldn't remember me, Samantha. But I can say this: you know my client."

Ishmael was an unusual-looking man. He seemed both comfortably relaxed and oddly uncomfortable. He often didn't know what to do with his hands, which sometimes hung straight down, or crossed over his chest. He radiated serenity, but every now and then, perplexingly, a black streak of darkness, like a worm, would weave through his beautiful, silver aura. Amazingly, my inner alarm system remained silent.

"And who's your client?" I asked.

He continued to watch me. Now, he held his hands together loosely at his waist. I think the guy would have been better off utilizing his pants pockets. Another streak of blackness flashed through his aura, so fast that I nearly didn't see it. Then another.

He smiled at me in a way that few men have ever smiled at me: knowingly, lovingly, comfortably, happily, sexily.

Finally, he said, "The client, Sam, was you."

4.

We had spent the evening baking cookies and generally making a mess of the kitchen. Flour, cinnamon, sprinkles, and sugar dusted the floor, our three sets of footprints overlapping on the tile, like some mad Family Circus diagram. But what's Christmas for, if not to bake with children?

Then we all cuddled up on the couch. I had put in the *Groundhog Day* DVD and we watched it with a fresh batch of cookies and milk. Of course, I only pretended to eat my cookies, which I promptly spit back into my milk. Ah, but those few seconds of sugary delight were heaven...but I would pay a price for it...Anything not blood, no matter how minute, would cause me severe cramping and the dry heaves later.

When the kids were in bed and I had gotten caught up on my office paperwork and billing, I grabbed my laptop and curled up on one corner of the living room couch.

You there, Fang?

No doubt, other creatures of the night were out running around...doing whatever it was that creatures of the night do. I knew what I did. I worked. And besides, tonight was a school night. And, despite being a professional private investigator who works the late shift, I couldn't leave my kids alone at night unless I could find a sitter.

That was why being married had been so convenient. Danny, my ex-husband, would watch the kids while I worked late. That is, until he started staying late himself, for reasons that weren't so admirable.

I drummed my fingers along the laptop case, waiting for Fang to reply. At the far end of the hallway, I could hear Anthony snoring lightly, even through his closed door. Along with my condition came an increased perception of many of my senses. Hearing and sight were two of them. I could hear and see things that I had no business hearing and seeing. The sense of taste and touch, not so much, which was just as well.

I couldn't eat food anyway, and I certainly didn't need inadvertent orgasms every time someone touched my shoulder. The jury was still out on my sense of smell, although it might have increased a little. Not necessarily a good thing with a gaseous eight-year-old around. Anyway, I had always had a good sniffer, so it was kind of hard to tell for sure.

Ah...there he was. The little pencil icon appeared in the chatbox window, indicating that Fang was typing a response.

Good evening, Moon Dance. Or, more accurately, good middle-of-the-night.

Good middle-of-the-night to you, too.

He typed a smiley face, followed by: *So, to what do I owe the pleasure of your company, Moon Dance?*

Fang was my online confidant. He was also a convicted murderer and escaped convict with serious psychological issues. But that's another story for another time. Over the years, though, he had proven to be loyal, knowledgeable and extremely helpful. After six years of anonymously chatting, Fang and I had finally met for the first time six months ago. The meeting had been interesting, and there had been some physical chemistry.

But then came "The Request."

Again, six months ago, back when my son

was losing his battle with the extremely rare Kawasaki disease, Fang had asked me to turn him into a vampire.

Now, that's a helluva request, even among close friends. At the time I was dealing with too much and had told him so. He understood. His timing was off. He got it. We hadn't discussed his request for a while now, but it was always out there, simmering, seething just below the current of all our conversations. We both knew it was out there. We both knew I would get around to it when the time was right.

And what would be my answer? I didn't know. Not yet. The question, for now, was bigger than I was. I need time to wrap my brain around it. To let it simmer. Percolate. Brew.

But someday, perhaps someday soon, I would give him my answer.

I wrote: *I have a question.*

You usually do, Fang replied.

What do you know of silver auras?

They're common, although they're usually associated with other colors, why?

I saw a silver aura today, but a bright one. Perhaps the brightest I'd ever seen. A radiant, glorious silver.

No other colors?

I shook my head, even though he couldn't see me shaking my head. *Just silver,* I typed.

Hang on.

There was a long pause, and I suspected Fang was either thinking or Googling or consulting what I knew to be a vast, private occult library. I knew something of occult libraries...having met a curious young curator of such a library, six months ago.

I waited. My house was mostly silently, other than Anthony's light snoring. Was it normal for an eight-year-old to snore? I wondered if I should have that checked. These days, after the ordeal with Kawasaki disease, I was constantly on guard with Anthony's health.

Fang came back, typing: *Please describe him to me, Moon Dance.*

Tallish, I wrote. *Well-built. Narrow waist. Broad shoulders. Smiled a lot.*

What did he say to you?

I thought about that. *Said he knew me, and had known me from way back, that he worked with me...or implied that he had worked with me. He knew my name.*

But did you recognize him?

No.

What about your inner alarm system? Did he trigger it? Were you on guard?

Quite the opposite, I wrote. *If anything, I felt at peace.*

There was a long delay, then finally, Fang's

words appeared in the IM chat box:

Unless I'm mistaken, Moon Dance, I believe you just met your guardian angel.

5.

Charlie lived in a single-wide trailer.

Although the trailer looked old, it appeared well-enough maintained. As I approached the door in the late evening, I realized that I had never been inside a single-wide trailer.

Somehow, I controlled my excitement.

The exterior was composed of metal siding, and there was a lot of junk piled around the house. Controlled junk, as it was mostly on old tables and shelving. Lawn mower parts, fan belts, engine parts, and just about everything else that belonged in a garage, except the mobile home didn't have a garage.

The front door was, in fact, a sliding glass door. Charlie, apparently, used the mobile home's rear door as his front door. A quick glance around the home explained why: the front door had no steps leading up to it.

Leading up to the sliding glass door was a small wooden deck, which I used now. I peered inside. It was the living room, and where the exterior had controlled mayhem, the interior was a straight-up mess. Charlie Anderson, it appeared, was a hoarder. The shelving theme from outside was extended to the inside. Shelves lined the walls, packed with plastic containers, themselves filled with computer parts, cables, and other electronic doodads. Interestingly, not a single book lined his book shelves. The floor was stacked with newspapers and speakers and car radios and old computer towers in various stages of disarray. Boxes were piled everywhere. And not neatly. Dog toys and old bones littered the floor. A huge TV sat in the far corner of the room, draped in a blanket, while a much smaller TV sat next to it, currently showing something science-fictiony. Zombies or robots, or both.

I was just about to knock on the glass door when a fat little white terrier sprang from the couch and charged me, barking furiously. All teeth and chub. But at the door, it suddenly pulled up, stopped barking, and looked at me curiously. I looked back at it. It cocked its head to one side. I didn't cock my head.

Then it whimpered and dashed off.

As it did so, I heard more movement...the sound of someone getting out of a recliner, followed by Charlie Anderson's happy-go-lucky, round face.

He let me in, asking if I'd found the place okay. I assured him I had. Once inside, I could fully appreciate just how much crap Charlie had. And yet...I had a sneaking suspicion that Charlie knew exactly where all his junk was.

"Nice place you have here." I was speaking facetiously, and a little in awe, too.

But Charlie took it as a real compliment, bless his heart.

"Thanks, but it's just home. I used to worry about cleaning and stuff like that, but I figured what's the point? My friends call me a hoarder, but I just like junk. I think there's a difference."

"Sure," I said.

He looked at me eagerly. "So, you agree there's a difference?"

I could tell he wanted me to agree, to confirm that he didn't have a hoarding problem, that he was just another guy with thousands of glass jars stacked on a long shelf over his kitchen table. The jars, as far as I could tell, were filled with every conceivable nut and bolt known to man. Thank God they weren't filled with human hearts. I leaned over. The jar closest to me was filled with—and I had to do a double take here—*bent* nails.

"Yes," I said. "There's a huge difference."

Charlie exhaled, relieved. I think we might have just bonded a little. "I think so, too," he said, nodding enthusiastically. "Would you like a Diet Pepsi?"

"I'm okay."

"Water?"

"I'm fine. Maybe you can show me where you kept the safe, Charlie?"

"Oh, yes. Right this way."

He led me through his many stacks of random junk. We even stepped around an old car fender. A fender. Seriously? Laying next to the fender was the upper half of a desk, the half with the doors that no one ever uses. There was no sign of the lower half anywhere. Just the upper. Seriously?

But there was more. So much more.

The junk seemed eternal. I already felt lost, consumed. How anyone could live like this, I didn't know. The junk almost seemed to take on a life of its own, as if it was the real inhabitant of the house, and we were the strangers, the trespassers. Indeed, I could even see the chaotic energy, bright and pulsating, swirling throughout the house. Crazy, frenetic energy that seemed trapped and still-connected to the many inanimate objects.

Energy, I knew, could attach to an object, especially an object of great importance, and so, really, I wasn't too surprised to see the spirit of the old woman hanging around an even older-looking piano. Granted, the piano itself was mostly covered in junk, but the old woman didn't seem to care much about that.

"Where did you get this piano?" I asked.

As I spoke, the old woman, who had mostly been ignoring us, turned and looked at me with some interest.

Charlie, who was about to lead the way down a narrow hallway, paused, and looked back. "My neighbor was throwing it out."

"Why?"

"He was moving. I guess it belonged to his mother, who was a music teacher, I think. She died a few years back. I shored up my floor with some extra jacks underneath and pushed it through the sliding glass door. It wasn't easy, but I got it in here."

"Do you play?" I asked.

"No."

"Have you ever, ah, heard it play before?"

"What do you mean?"

"I mean, have you ever heard it play on its own?"

He looked at me, seemed to think about, or, more accurately, decide how much he wanted to tell me, then finally nodded. “Yeah, sometimes. Just a few notes. I figure it’s mice.”

“Do you believe in ghosts?” I asked. As I did so, the old lady drifted up from the piano seat where she’d been sitting along with some stacks of automobile manuals.

“Why do you ask?”

The woman approached me carefully. She was composed of a thousands, if not millions of staticky, supernatural filaments of super-bright light. Sometimes the filaments dispersed a little. When they did, she grew less distinct. Sometimes they came together tightly, and when they did, she took on more form, more details. As she approached, I could see where light pulsated brightly at the side of her head, and knew that she had died of a brain aneurysm. She reached out a hand, which looked so bright and detailed that it could have been physical. I reached out my own and took hers, and as I did so, a shiver coursed through me.

In that moment, I had an image of a school, with many dozens of children playing this very piano.

“No reason,” I said. “But, wouldn’t you think this piano would do some kids some good? Maybe at an elementary school?”

Charlie blinked hard, thought about that. Giving up his junk, I knew, was a torturous act. He shrugged. "Yeah, I suppose."

"Would you do that for me?"

He shrugged again. "Sure. But why?"

The old woman, who was still holding my hand, had covered her face with her other hand. Shivers continued up and down my arm. "Seems the right thing to do, doesn't it?"

Charlie shrugged. "Yeah, I suppose so. I am sort of worried about the floor. Even with the extra jacks underneath. I'll do it tomorrow. I can check around with some schools."

"You're a good man, Charlie Brown."

He smiled and turned a little red. I released the old woman's hand, who smiled and drifted back to the piano. As I did so, I had a thought, "When did you acquire the piano?"

"Last week."

"Before or after the theft of the safe?"

"After. Why?"

Ghosts, I knew from firsthand experience, made for excellent witnesses. Unfortunately, the timing didn't line up here. "No reason," I said.

Charlie studied me, shrugged for the millionth time, and led me over to the furnace, which was located about halfway down the hallway. Once there, he removed the metal cover, set it down, and grabbed a flashlight from the nearby bathroom.

"I kept the safe in here," he said, and shined the light at an empty space above the furnace. "I just set it in there."

"It wasn't bolted in?"

"No. It's heavy, but so's the furnace. The safe just sat right where the old blower used to be. The thing broke ages ago. That's it right over there."

He pointed the flashlight over to a dome-shaped, metal-encased fan. Surrounding the fan were a lot of old baggies full of random screws and washers. One of the baggies even had baggies in it. Hoarding at its purest.

"Can you give me a minute alone?" I asked.

"Sure...you gonna dust for prints or something?"

"Or something," I said.

He nodded and smiled eagerly, anything to please me. No doubt anything to please anyone. He stepped back through his labyrinthine hallway, contorting his body this way and that, and when he was gone, I went to work.

6.

First, I scanned the hallway.

I noted a window directly opposite the furnace. The window was covered by both blinds and a curtain. Upon closer inspection, I saw that the blind wasn't really made for this window. It was a half inch too narrow...perhaps just narrow enough for someone to see through.

I next ran my fingers along the dusty curtain, and what struck me immediately was how thin the material was. Thin and see-through. Individually, the blinds were too narrow and the curtains too thin. But together, they should have done the job of keeping away prying eyes.

I thought about that as I scanned his hallway

...and spotted the oscillating fan at the end. The fan was turned off, but I had another thought.

I went over to it and turned it on. It faced into what appeared to be Charlie's bedroom. Then it started oscillating, turning briefly toward the hallway. The blast of air from the fan wasn't much. But it was enough. A moment later, the hem of the curtain fluttered up.

I watched three or four revolutions of the fan, and each time, the hem of the curtain fluttered higher and higher. I went back to the window and studied it, and as I studied it, an image began to form in my thoughts.

The image coalesced into that of a young man standing just outside the window. I closed my eyes and the image came into sharper focus. A young man who was watching Charlie. Standing just outside the trailer. Late at night.

Who the person was, I hadn't a clue. Why he happened to be standing just outside the trailer, I didn't know that either. My psychic hits are just that. Hits. Not all-knowing information. Glimpses of information. Snapshots of information. It was up to me to dig deeper, to decipher, to probe, and ultimately to figure out what the hell it all meant.

I went back into the living room, walked around the upper half of a recliner—just the upper half, mind you—and found Charlie scratching his fat little pooch. The dog saw me, promptly piddled on the carpet, and dashed off into the kitchen. Or what should have been a kitchen. In Charlie's world, it was just another storage room.

"Rocko!" he shouted, but Charlie didn't really sound angry. He sounded shocked, if anything. He immediately produced a rag from somewhere on his person and went to work on the pee stain in the carpet. "I don't know what's gotten into him."

"Maybe he smells my sister's cat on me," I said, since it seemed safer to say than: *It's probably because I'm a blood-sucking fiend, and dogs, for some reason, can sense us.*

"Maybe," said Charlie. "But dogs are going to be dogs, ya know? You can't get mad at them for being dogs."

I smiled at his simple philosophy. I asked, "Do you ever leave Rocko alone?"

"Sometimes, but he likes to ride in the car with me."

"So there are times when your house is completely empty?"

"I suppose so, yeah."

As he cleaned, I asked him how often he checked on the safe. He looked up at me from the floor, a little sweat already appearing on his brow as he worked at the dog pee. "Well, I don't really check it."

"What do you do?"

He looked away, suddenly embarrassed. He stopped scrubbing the floor. His balding head gleamed. "I guess I sometimes look at it."

"Look at it?"

He thought some more. "Well, I guess it reminds me of my dad, you know? And my grandfather. We all had the at one time or another. We all talked about it. And sometimes..." But Charlie suddenly got choked up and couldn't continue.

So I finished for him. "And sometimes when you looked at it, or when you touched it, you could feel your father and grandfather nearby."

Charlie wiped his eyes and nodded and looked away.

7.

Admittedly, the blood wasn't very Christmassy.

It was late and I was alone in my office with a packet of the good stuff, freshly delivered today from the slaughterhouse in Norco. As I slit open the top of the plastic bag with a fingernail that was a little too thick and a little too sharp, I reflected on what I knew about blood.

Fresh blood energized me, lifted me, made me feel more than human. With fresh blood flowing through my veins, I felt like I could do anything. And for all I knew, maybe I could.

Acquiring fresh blood is another issue altogether.

I'm not a killer, although I have killed. To drink fresh blood implies two things: it has either been taken...or freely given. The freely given part was a concept I was still wrapping my brain around. One of the perks of dating Kingsley these past few months was that he always kept a fresh supply of hemoglobin for me. Where he got it, I may never know, and he wasn't telling. All I knew was that it made me feel like a new woman. Hell, like a new species.

But I will not take blood unwillingly from humans, although I certainly could if I wanted to. I imagined there were others like me out there who took from others when and where they wanted it. I suspected that many of the missing person cases around the world were a result of this, although I could be wrong, since I'm not exactly immersed in the vampire sub-culture. I'm immersed in my kids and school and work, and dealing with an ex-husband who had revamped his efforts to bring me down. How he would do this, I don't know, but if ever there was someone who ran hot and cold, it was Danny.

Bi-polar, as my sister put it.

I studied the semi-clear packet of blood. The packet was no bigger than my hand. I didn't need much blood, and a packet this size would keep me going for three or four days. I didn't need to drink nightly, although I could, if I chose to. As I studied the packet, a thick animal hair rotated slowly within. Shuddering, I fished it out and flicked it in the waste basket.

Blech.

Hating my life, I brought the packet to my mouth, tilted it up, and drank deeply as the thick blood filled my mouth. I ignored the bigger chunks of flesh, and only gagged two times. I kept drinking until the packet was empty, until I'd squeezed out every last drop.

When I did, I shuddered and closed my eyes and willed the blood to stay down. I kept my fist over my mouth and kept shuddering. When I opened my eyes, I saw him standing there, in the far corner of my office, watching me.

The man from the dollar store.

Or, as Fang put it...my guardian angel.

8.

I gasped.

I might be a creature of the night, but that doesn't mean I don't get startled. My first instinct was to dash toward the door of my office, which is what I did, blocking the stranger from further access into my house. One moment I was sitting at my desk, downing a packet of cow blood, gagging, and the next, I was standing guard at my office door.

"I didn't mean to startle you, Samantha."

"Of course not, asshole. Which is why you appeared suddenly in my office. You have five seconds before I throw you through that wall."

I was a mixture of rage and confusion. The adrenaline-fueled rage for obvious reasons. The confusion because my inner alarm system had been completely bypassed. What the hell was going on?

I kept an ear out towards my kids, listening hard, but all I could hear was Anthony's light snoring. Tammy wasn't snoring, but I could sense her there in her room, curled up in her bed, one arm tucked under her pillow.

"Your extrasensory skills are progressing rapidly, Samantha."

"What do you mean?" I asked, perplexed, angered, wracking my brain for an explanation of how he had appeared so suddenly in my office. I found none.

He watched me from the corner of the room, hands folded in front of him, smiling serenely. His blondish hair seemed to lift and fall on currents of air that I sure as hell didn't feel.

He cocked his head slightly to one side. "Your image of your sleeping daughter, of course. Your psychic hit is completely accurate."

At any other time I might have rushed the guy. At the least, slamming him up against the wall to get some straight answers. But I held back. For now.

"Who the hell are you, goddammit?" I asked.

"God never damns, Samantha."

"You'd better start talking, mister. Or Ishmael. Or whoever the hell you are."

He smiled again, so warmly that at any other time, he might have won me over. Any other time, that is, other than appearing in my office in the dead of night, while seemingly knowing the details of my sleeping daughter.

"Who do you think I am, Samantha?" he asked.

"A dead man, unless you start talking."

His hair, which hung just over his ears, lifted and fell again, and I was beginning to wonder if I was dreaming. The light particles that formed brilliantly around him seemed to disappear *into* him, which was a first to me.

"You have grown stronger over these past seven years...and more violent, too. The violence is part of your nature now, I suppose, but my hope is that you learn to suppress it. Violence has a way of getting out of control, controlling you." He stepped slowly out of the shadows of my office, away from the bookcase, and stepped around my old recliner. When I don't use the office for work, it's my escape from my kids, where I come to read...or sometimes just to cry, although no one knows about the crying.

"Who are you?" I asked again.

"I am that which you think I am, Samantha."

"How do you know what I'm thinking?"

He smiled, but did not answer.

I waited. He waited. My conversation with Fang came roaring back. I shook my head in disbelief. Ishmael smiled even broader and held out his hands a little.

"You're my guardian angel?" I said, unable to hide the disbelief from my voice.

He continuing smiling as he stepped around my recliner. "You sound incredulous, Sam. This coming from someone such as yourself."

"Such as myself? And what would that be? Exactly?"

"A vampire, Samantha Moon. At least, that's what this present generation calls your condition. It has, of course, been called many other things, over many centuries. Admittedly, the curse has flared darker and stronger in this generation."

"I don't understand."

"When enough people speak of something, read of something, believe in something, watch something, ingest something...this something begins to take on a life of its own. This something is called into existence."

My head was spinning. "Called into existence from where?"

"From the nether-sphere, Sam. From out there. From the great soup of all ideas and thoughts and creative expressions."

He continued toward me and I held up my hand. "I think you should stop right there."

He did stop. Next to one of my client chairs. "I will not hurt you, Sam. It's against my very nature to hurt you. In fact, quite the opposite."

"Opposite?"

He nodded once, sharply. "My nature is to protect you."

"Because you're my guardian angel."

"Yes, Sam. Because I'm your guardian angel."

9.

“Perhaps we can sit and I can explain,” he said. “Your children are safe. Perhaps more safe than you know.”

I stared at his pleasantly handsome face as he regarded me in turn. His bright green eyes could have been emerald flames, if such things existed. He radiated waves of strength and confidence and...love. My mind reeled.

“Okay, let’s sit,” I said finally.

We did so, he in one of my client chairs, myself behind my desk. Ishmael was wearing a light-colored sweater and slacks. Both were unremarkable, although both looked good on him. He sat collected and at ease, his hands folded loosely in his lap. He looked at me calmly, staring into my eyes, although sometimes his eyes would shift to take in other aspects of my face. A small part of me wondered what my hair looked like.

"So," I said, "they call you Ishmael."

His eyes, which shone like twin sparks of emerald fire, flashed brightly with mild amusement. "Yes, they do."

I watched with interest as the bright streaks of light that seemingly only I could see, the bright streaks that illuminated the night world for my eyes, flared brightly the closer they got to him. Flared, and then disappeared into him. As if the being seated across from me was the source of the light.

Or perhaps its destination.

"So, why are you here, Ishmael?"

He sat perfectly still, perfectly composed, perfectly at ease. He nodded once before he spoke. "I'm here, in part, to tell you that my service is no longer needed."

"And what service is that?"

"The protective service."

My cell phone chimed. I had a text message from someone. At this late hour, it was either from Fang or Kingsley. I ignored it. Truth be known, I kept waiting to either wake up or be told that this was all some big practical joke.

In the meantime, I noted that Ishmael's thoughts were closed to me. In my experience, only other immortals were closed to me, as I was to them. And yet, he seemed to have read my mind.

I tried an experiment and thought: *You're in the protective services because you're a guardian angel?*

His bright green eyes, which had been regarding me serenely from across the desk, widened a little. "Yes, Sam. But we don't call ourselves guardian angels."

You can read my thoughts.

He smiled. "Of course."

To date, only Fang had access to my thoughts, and even then his access seemed limited by my willingness to let him in. Kingsley, a fellow freak, did not have access, nor did I have access to his. Same with the few other immortals I had encountered, who were all closed off to me.

"So, there are others like you?" I asked.

"Of course."

"And what do you call yourselves?"

"We are watchers."

I nodded. "And what do you watch?"

"I watch you, Sam."

"Just watch?"

"Watch and protect and guide."

"Then you've done a shitty job of it," I said suddenly, thinking of my attack seven years ago.

Ishmael kept his eyes on me. After a moment, he said, "I was with you, Sam. Always with you."

"Even while that animal attacked me?" I couldn't help the anger in my voice.

Ishmael said nothing at first, although he slowly raised a hand to his face and rubbed his jaw. He continued to stare at me. Even his minor movements were fluid and hypnotic. "Perhaps you wonder why you were not killed that night, Sam."

"Actually, I do."

"Perhaps you should know that your attacker ended many lives, Samantha. He would have ended yours, too. In fact, he was just seconds from doing so."

The so-called watcher lapsed into silence and continued rubbing his jaw. The physical movement seemed to intrigue him, and now he slowly ran his hand over his own soft lips, feeling them, using his fingertips as a painter would a sable-tipped brush. I had the impression Ishmael rarely manifested in the physical.

I was about to speak, but suddenly found

speaking difficult. I was back to that moment in the park, experiencing again the ungodly strength of the thing that had attacked me, the blast of pain of being hurled against a tree...the fear of being pounced on by something so much stronger than me. Yes, I should have been dead many times over. So, instead of speaking, I thought: *You saved me.*

Ishmael briefly paused in his exploration of his face. "It wasn't your time."

"Then why let me get attacked at all? Why let me get turned into...this thing?"

"Fair questions, Sam, but we are not quite the guardian angels as you think of us. Not the static lighted angel on top of your Christmas tree, assembled by small children in an Asian country. Not the Michelangelo-ish ones painted on ceilings of cathedrals or glorified in Christmas carols and hymns galore. Not the ones in old movies on TV, getting our wings every time someone rings a bell. Not those angels. *Not.*"

"Then what the hell are you?"

"Think of us as custodians of destiny."

I blinked, processing that. "You help fulfill destinies?"

He nodded. "I helped you fulfill your destiny, Sam."

"And my destiny was to become a vampire?"

"Your destiny was to become immortal. Vampirism was one way to achieve that."

"So, I chose this life?"

"You did."

"Why?"

"I'm not at liberty to say."

"Why not?"

"You are not ready for the answer."

I fought through my frustration. "Will I ever find the answer?"

"Yes, someday."

I drummed my fingers along my desk, my thick nails clicking loudly. They sounded fiendish, like the claws of something dark and slimy moving quickly over the floor. I said, "So, in effect, the moment I turned into a vampire, the moment I became immortal myself, you were out of a job."

"That's correct, Sam."

"So, what have you been doing these past seven years?"

"Watching you, Sam. Always watching you."

"Why?"

He looked away, and as he did so, he looked very, very human. And even a little uncomfortable. He kept looking away as he spoke. "Because I'm in love with you, Samantha Moon."

10.

You there, Fang?

I'm always here for you, Moon Dance.

Oh, cut the crap. Half the time, you've got a woman over there.

Not as frequently as you think, Moon Dance. And not since we've met.

But that was over six months ago.

It was.

But why?

It seems the right thing to do. Besides, I've lost interest in dating in general.

Since you met me?

That might have something to do with it, Moon Dance. But don't flatter yourself. Perhaps it was time for me to slow down, to take stock of who I am and what I want in life.

You want to be a vampire.

There was a short pause before he wrote: *Among other things.*

I did not have to dip very far into Fang's mind to know he was referring to me. Truth be known, I didn't much enjoy dipping into Fang's mind. His mind was not healthy, although he was doing an admirable job of dealing with his many issues. I found it ironic that the one mind I was most linked to was a deeply troubled one.

I felt him probing my mind in return and let him do it, giving him access of the events of the night before. A moment later, his words appeared in the IM chat box.

You have got to be kidding, Moon Dance.

I'm not.

Now I have to compete with a freakin' angel, too?

Despite myself, I laughed. I wrote: *You're not competing with anyone, Fang. I'm with Kingsley. Happily with Kingsley.*

Is that what you told Captain Ahab?

Ishmael, I wrote. *And yes. After I spent about three minutes getting over my shock...and another two minutes convincing myself I wasn't dreaming, I told him I was happily with Kingsley.*

And how did he take it?

He laughed and said he was infinitely patient, that we had all eternity.

Since when do angels cavort with vampires?

He calls himself a watcher.

Either way. I don't like it, Moon Dance.

I didn't think you would.

I need to look into this.

I figured you would.

Was he handsome?

I thought about it, still reeling from the encounter, still wondering if this was all some elaborate practical joke, and, as always, still wondering if I was still back at the hospital, lying comatose after my attack seven years ago. For now, though, I recalled Ishmael's emerald eyes and quiet strength...and the love that emanated from him seemingly unconditionally.

I thought about it some more, then wrote: *He was radiant.*

Ah, shit.

11.

I was back at Charlie's single-wide mobile home. Or, rather, standing just outside it.

It was evening and the mobile home park was mostly quiet. I could smell fish frying and meats baking. TV sets glowed in many of the mobile homes. Outside the window in question, where the blinds were a little too narrow and the curtains were a little too thin, I paused and took in the scene.

The area between Charlie's home and the home next to his was covered in white gravel and seemed to serve as a small parking lot. There was also a path that led between the two homes. The path seemed to connect one side of the park to the other. The path led just outside the window in question.

Amazingly, there were no flood lights here, and the whole space was blanketed in darkness. It would have been easy enough for someone to pause outside the window and watch Charlie with his safe.

A narrow road curved through the mobile home park, which cars occasionally sped along, heedless of children, pets, Santa's reindeer or vampires.

The question was: who had been watching Charlie?

Still standing next to Charlie's mobile home, listening to a cacophony of "It's a Holly, Jolly Christmas," TV news anchormen, video game explosions and the clanking of dishes, I closed my eyes and expanded my consciousness out through the park. A trick I had learned a few months ago. In my mind's eye, I saw glimpses of men in Christmas tree print boxers, women in tubs of vanilla bubbles, most of them shaving their legs, and even an older couple getting frisky under the covers. I saw teens playing Xbox and even grown men playing Xbox. I saw men and women talking excitedly, passionately, agitatedly. I saw children crying and playing, but mostly crying and being warned that Santa was still making his list of naughty and nice children. I saw sumptuous dinners being eaten in front of TVs tuned into Donna Reed and Jimmy Stewart but rarely at dinner tables. Gather round the TV, all ye faithful.

I also saw four young men sitting together in the living room of one of the nearby double wide mobile homes. The young men were sitting around bags of weed and the occasional bag of crack cocaine. I saw guns in waistbands and a lot of bad attitudes. There was no sign of Christmas in their house, nor Hanukkah, nor Kwanzaa. A dead giveaway, for sure. No holiday cheer or spirit at all. Of any sort.

My consciousness snapped back, leaving me briefly discombobulated. What I hadn't seen was the stolen safe, but I figured the drug dealers' home was as good a place to start as any.

12.

I knocked on the drug dealers' front door.

I listened with a small grin to the frantic sounds of weed and crack being hidden in everything from toilets to cookie jars, to no doubt deep inside boxers and briefs. I heard a chair fall over. I heard someone curse under his breath. I heard the sounds of shushing and the running of footsteps.

I was tempted to yell, "Police" and really listen to the fireworks within. I might even hear a window crash as one of them makes a run for it.

Instead, I waited, rocking gently back and forth, hands behind my back, just a five foot, three-inch mother of two confronting your neighborhood drug dealers.

My alarm system was jangling, but I mostly ignored it. I knew, after all, what I was walking into.

Finally, I heard footsteps cautiously approach the door.

An acne-covered Caucasian face peered at me through the door's dirty curtain. The face frowned, and then looked almost comically left and right before he partially opened the door.

"Excuse me," I said. "But my car broke down and I was wondering if I could borrow your phone?"

"My phone? Yo, fuck off, bitch. This ain't no Triple Fucking A." And he promptly slammed the door in my face.

Or tried to.

I stuck out my hand, and the door rebounded off it so hard that it slammed back into the drug dealer's face. I followed the swinging door in, pushing harder. The young punk reached for his nose and for something under his shirt. And since I didn't feel like getting shot tonight, I caught his hand in mid-reach, twisted until he dropped to both knees, and grabbed what he'd been reaching for under his shirt.

I came away with a Smith & Wesson revolver.

I swung the gun around and pointed it at the

others, who were all reaching inside their own pants. Apparently, this was the official greeting of drug dealers everywhere.

"Hello, boys," I said. "Hands where I can see them."

"Fuck this shit," said a tall black kid who couldn't have been more than eighteen. He pulled up his shirt, revealing the gleaming walnut handle of an expensive revolver, and before his hand got very far beyond that, I fired the weapon. A bullet hole appeared in the kitchen linoleum next to his foot, perhaps just inches away.

He jumped maybe three feet, screaming like a girl. "Holy sweet Jesus! The bitch is crazy!"

I held the gun steady on the trio who were standing around the kitchen table. All three were in their late teens or early twenties. Hardly drug lords.

I said, "Next one who calls me a bitch gets a bullet in their big toe. Got it?"

No one moved or said anything. The guy next to me whimpered a little, and I realized I was still twisting his arm. I let him go and threw him a little at the same time. He skidded across the kitchen floor. Okay, I might have thrown him *a lot*.

I next had them drop their guns and kick them over to me. Once done, I gathered the weapons and emptied them of their bullets. I dropped the bullets in one of my jacket pockets. Next, I had the four hoodlums sit around the kitchen table like good little boys.

Or bad boys.

They didn't like a woman telling them what to do. Myself, I was getting a kick out of it. When they were all seated and staring at me sullenly, I hopped up on a stool and held the gun casually in front of me. I couldn't help but notice my feet not only didn't reach the floor, they didn't even reach the first rung of the stool. Still, I swung them happily and looked at my four new friends.

"Well," I said, "here we all are."

The oldest of the four, a Hispanic guy with a tattoo on his neck, leaned forward on his elbows. "Fuck you, bi—" But he stopped himself.

"Nice catch," I said. "You just saved yourself a big toe. Merry Christmas from me."

It was all the guy could do to stay seated. I sensed he wanted to rush me. In fact, I was sure of it. Every now and then, he caught the eye of the black guy across from him. Something passed between them. I didn't care what passed between them.

For now, though, he needed more information, like who the hell I was, and so he stayed seated. For now.

"You ain't no cop," he said.

"Nope."

"You with the feds?"

"Used to be."

"Then what the hell are you?"

"That's the million-dollar question."

They all looked at each other. Two of them shrugged. From the living room, I heard the *Jeopardy* theme song. I was willing to bet that drug dealers the world over had *Jeopardy* playing in the background. Nothing so innocent as four hoodlums watching *Jeopardy* together.

The Caucasian kid who had greeted me at the door had yet to look me in the eye. He stared down at the table. His wrist was raw and red where I had subdued him. He knew the potential of my strength, and kept his eyes off me and his mouth shut. The fourth guy was another black youth, maybe twenty. He had yet to speak, although he found all of this highly amusing. I sensed he was high as a kite. If I was high as a kite, I would find all this amusing, too. I focused on the Hispanic leader and the talkative black guy.

I said, "Somebody stole something that belonged to me, and I want it back." Technically, that was true, since half of whatever was in the safe was now mine.

"We lovers," said the talkative black guy. "Not thieves."

The high-as-a-kite black guy laughed. The Hispanic guy frowned. The sullen white guy kept being sullen.

"Cut the shit," I said. "I know there's drugs here." I pointed to a Pillsbury Doughboy cookie jar with a crack running up along its doughy body. "I know there're drugs in that cookie jar over there. I know there're drugs in the toilet bowl, and I know there're drugs down all your pants."

The high-as-a-kite black guy giggled nearly uncontrollably. The Hispanic leader sat forward. The energy around him crackled and spat. He said, "What the fuck do you want, lady?"

"I want the safe," I said.

"What safe?"

As I said those words, I watched the others in the room. The talkative black guy blinked. The high black guy continued grinning from ear to ear. The sullen white guy sank a little deeper in his chair. Just a little. Perhaps only a fraction. Not to mention his darkish aura grew darker still.

I had my man.

It was at that moment that I saw the old man in the far corner of the living room. Correction, two old men, as another just materialized. And they weren't exactly men.

They were ghosts.

13.

I jumped off the stool.

As I did so, the Hispanic guy made a move to stand. He didn't move very far. A casual backhand across his face sent him spinning sideways to the floor. The others stayed seated, which wasn't a bad idea. I told them not to move and they mostly didn't, although the high-as-a-kite guy continued to fight through a case of the giggles.

I moved past them, slipping the gun inside my waistband. The backhand smack to their leader would keep the trio quiet for a few minutes.

People don't realize that spirits tend to be just about everywhere. I see them appearing and disappearing almost continuously, sometimes randomly. I'll see them briefly materialize by someone's side, squeeze their hand or hug them, and then flit off again. Usually the object of such affection is left shivering pleasantly. No doubt, the unseen encounter suddenly brought an unexpected memory to the recipient.

And some spirits, like the old lady and her piano, attach themselves to objects, seemingly for decades, although I always suspected that only an aspect of their spirit attached. The majority of their spirit was elsewhere, wherever spirits might go.

Then again, I could be wrong.

As I approached the two old men, they turned toward me. Their attention, I saw, had been centered around something in the far corner of the room, something hidden under a blanket. The spirits themselves were formed of bright filaments of light that coalesced to form shapes. In this case, the shapes of two older men.

They didn't speak and their shapes were only vaguely held together, which suggested to me that these were older spirits. Older, as in having died long ago.

Charlie had said that his father had died nearly two decades ago...and no doubt his grandfather had died many years before that.

His grandfather and father were certainly two spirits who would have been powerfully connected to an object.

The safe.

The corner of this room smelled of smoke, or of something burned, and as I got closer, I saw tools scattered around the living room that didn't belong there. Hammers. Mallets. Crowbars. Even a blowtorch. The corner of the couch was blackened, too, but that's what happens when you use a blowtorch indoors.

I had the attention of both spirits, who watched me closely, silently, as I reached down and pulled back the corner of a stained quilt, revealing a very old-looking and heavy safe, the lock of which had been blackened by the blowtorch.

But the safe was still locked...and that's all that mattered.

14.

As tomorrow was Christmas Eve, I thought it a fitting gift when I delivered the safe to Charlie's door.

Orange County doesn't get snow. Hell, we rarely get rain, but as I approached the door, carrying the safe under one arm, a stiff, cool breeze appeared, and that was good enough. Any weather was good enough at this time of the year.

I knocked on his door to the rhythm of "Jingle bells, jingle bells, jingle all the way" and fat little Rocko jumped from the couch, barking his brains out, until he got a look at me, then he hit the brakes, and scuttled off with his tail between his legs. Thank God Kingsley didn't have the same reaction.

I set the safe down on the wooden deck, noting how the wood sagged mightily under the weight of the safe.

Charlie's round face soon appeared and he gave me a big smile. Charlie, I saw, needed some serious dental work. Except he didn't seem to care that he needed dental work, or that his teeth looked like crooked tombstones. Charlie was just happy to be Charlie.

He was about to slide open his door when he glanced down, and his crooked smile seemed to freeze in place. He blinked. Hard.

Then threw open the door.

I shouldn't have been surprised when he gave me the mother of all hugs, but I was.

***

We were in his living room.

I had told him that a friend of mine had helped me lug the heavy safe onto his deck, and I made a show of pretending to struggle with the safe as we moved it from the deck to the center of his living room.

Amid leaning towers of laser jet printer cartridges, 40's science fiction magazines, and enough clipboards to last two lifetimes, we set the heavy safe down.

Earlier in the night, after my discovery of the safe, I gave the boys ten minutes to clear out before I called the police. Most were gone in five. I kept their weapons and ammunition, which I would hand over to Detective Sherbet of the Fullerton Police Department.

For now, though, it was just me, Charlie and the safe. And inside, something, neither of us knew what.

The safe was clearly old. So old that it looked like it belonged on the back of a Wells Fargo stage coach. Part of the safe's dial still gleamed brightly, although most of it was covered in blackened soot from the blowtorch. The handle was badly dented, no doubt thanks to the various hammers I had seen lying around.

Still, the safe had held fast, and that's all that mattered.

Charlie stared down at it. So did I. My compensation was in that safe, whatever it might be. Could be gold. Could be old war bonds. Could be jewelry, gemstones or pirate booty, for all I knew.

I had been tempted to see if my own psychic gifts could penetrate the heavy steel safe, but I had resisted.

"I guess this is it, then," said Charlie. He didn't sound very enthusiastic.

"Do you know the combination?"

He pointed to the upper corner of the safe, where, upon closer inspection, I saw a number etched, 14. Two other numbers were etched into other corners, 29 and 63.

I said them out loud and he nodded. "Don't think of them as three numbers, think of them as six numbers. One, four, two, nine, six and three. With that in mind, what are the two lowest numbers?"

I glanced at them again. "One and two."

He nodded. "Good. And the next lowest?"

"Three and four."

"Good, good. And the two highest?"

"Six and nine."

"You got it," he said, giving me a half smile.

"Twelve, thirty-four and sixty-nine?"

He nodded. "You're the first person I've ever given the key to. Not even to my own son."

"How old's your son?"

"Twenty-one. But it's too soon to give him the key. My father gave it to me on his deathbed."

"I feel honored," I said, and meant it.

We stared at it some more. He made no move to open it, and I certainly wasn't about to. Somewhere down the hall, one of his piles of junk shifted, groaning, as boulders do in the deserts. The piano, I saw, was gone.

The light particles behind Charlie began

coagulating and taking on shape, and shortly, two very faint old men appeared behind him. I noticed the hair on Charlie's arm immediately stood on end, as his body registered the spiritual presence of his father and grandfather, even if his mind hadn't. Charlie absently rubbed his arms.

"Well, let's get on with it," he said, and reached down for the safe.

As he did so, I said, "You really don't want to open the safe, do you, Charlie?"

"I do. Really, I do. A deal's a deal, and I want to pay you. Your half."

"But wouldn't you rather pass it along to your own boy?"

"Without you, Ms. Moon, I would have nothing to pass on to my kid. Besides, it's really a silly tradition."

"No, it's not. It's about family."

"We've been keeping this thing going for years and it's impractical at best, like a joke from beyond the grave."

"I think it's an amazing tradition," I said.

He didn't say it, but his body language suggested he thought so, too. He said, "Well, it is kind of fun not knowing what's in this thing. I mean, it could be anything, right? But I suppose it's time to find out once and for all?"

He made a move for the safe again, but he

didn't get very far, mostly because I grabbed his wrist. He shivered at my cold touch.

I said, "This isn't right."

"A deal's a deal, Ms. Moon. Besides, I have no other way of repaying you."

I thought about that, then looked around. "Not true. You have enough junk to stock a dozen houses. There's got to be something in here that I want."

"What are you saying, Ms. Moon?"

"I'm saying, let me pick something out of your junk, and the safe is yours. Keep it in your family. Pass it along to your son."

He processed that information, and I saw the relief ripple through him and his shining aura. "Are you sure?"

"As sure as I've ever been."

"But aren't you a little bit curious what's in the safe?"

"More than you know," and as I said those words, I briefly closed my eyes, and expanded my consciousness throughout the room, and as I did so, two things made me gasp.

The first was the contents of the safe, which I saw clearly. The second was what I saw resting inside a wooden box deep under a pile of newspapers.

Charlie was watching me curiously. "Are you okay?"

"Er, yes," I said, then patted him on the shoulder. "I would suggest you find a much better place for your safe."

"I will."

"A very safe place."

"You think the contents are valuable?"

I thought of the two old spirits, Charlie's father and grandfather. I thought of Charlie's own son and the unique bond that kept the generations connected. The safe. I also saw in my mind's eye the tightly rolled vellum document that might just be the rarest of all American documents, a document signed by our founding fathers, centuries ago. A document thought to be lost...until now.

Then again, I could be wrong.

Next, I moved through the piles of junk and headed to the far corner of the room. There, I began moving aside old newspapers and magazines, until I finally uncovered an ornately carved box.

I picked it up carefully, my hands trembling.

Slowly, I opened the lid...

Unbelievable.

Inside was another golden medallion. This time, the three roses were cut from brilliant amethysts.

Charlie was looking over my shoulder. "Oh, that. I got it at an estate sale a while back. In

Fullerton. Get this, some old guy was murdered by some nut with a crossbow. Anyway, it's gold, I think. Probably worth a lot. I've been keeping it for a rainy day." He paused. "Truth be known, it kind of gives me the creeps. You can have it if you want."

I closed the lid and held out my hand. "Merry Christmas."

But Charlie had other designs on me. He wrapped me in a huge, smothering hug. "Merry Christmas, Ms. Moon!"

15.

With the box sitting safely on the seat next to me, I had just pulled out of Charlie's mobile home park when my cell rang. It was Fang.

"Merry Christmas," I said.

"That sounds odd coming from a vampire," said Fang.

"Why, because I'm a creature of the night?"

"Something like that."

"I'll remind you that Santa does his best work at night."

"Santa isn't real."

"I thought the same about vampires," I said. "And someone recently told me that if people believe in something hard enough and long enough, it becomes true."

Fang laughed. "Enough about Santa Claus. I've got news. Your watcher friend is likely a fallen angel."

"He's no demon, Fang."

"Have you ever met a demon, Moon Dance?"

"I don't know," I said, recalling meeting Kingsley in my hotel room when he had fully transformed into a werewolf. The thing living inside him was as close to a demon as I've ever met. "I just know he's not evil."

"At least not yet."

"What, exactly, is a fallen angel?"

"A spiritual being that no longer commits itself to helping others evolve. In fact, quite the opposite."

"A being who helps others devolve?"

"Close. A being who spreads fear. Living in fear, any kind of fear, separates the individual from the Creator."

My head began to throb. Headaches, for me, rarely lasted more than a few minutes. I chewed my lip and drove and didn't like any of this. I said, "And so, what, one day he decides to turn bad?"

"It probably wasn't just one day, Moon Dance. It had probably been a long time coming."

"He said he's no longer bound to me..."

"If he was your guardian angel, that makes sense. Why should one immortal protect another?"

"Now that he's not bound to me..."

"Right," said Fang, picking up on my thoughts. "Now that he's not bound to you, he's free to approach me. A sort of metaphysical loophole." Fang paused. "I had a thought, Moon Dance, and a not very pleasant one."

"Tell me."

"What if he *allowed* you to be attacked?"

"What do you mean?"

"What if he not only allowed you to be attacked, but he had planned the whole night?"

"But why?" But even as I asked the question, I knew the answer.

Fang voiced it for me. "To turn you, Moon Dance. To turn you into that which he could finally approach. Or that which he could finally love."

I shuddered as I drove on into the night, winding my way now through the streets of Yorba Linda. "But he said my destiny was to become immortal. To become a vampire."

"Perhaps. Or perhaps he wasn't telling you the truth."

"But isn't he, you know, obligated to protect me?"

"I don't know, Moon Dance. We're talking

about the spirit world, something I'm not privy to. But I am familiar with the concept of spirit guides and guardian angels. From my understanding, yes, such beings are generally there to guide and protect and nurture. Unless..."

"Unless what?" I asked.

"Unless they decide not to."

"A fallen angel," I said.

"Exactly."

16.

Christmas Day, late.

They were all here. Mary Lou, her husband and three kids. Her three kids were about Tammy's and Anthony's ages, and they mostly all got along. Except when playing video games. Then, all bets were off.

Kingsley was here, too, and he looked absolutely sumptuous in his thick sweater and scarf, which hung loosely over a chest that should be illegal in most states. Kingsley wasn't a slender man. He was thick and hulking and as yummy as they get.

Detective Sherbet and his lovely Hungarian wife swung by to say hello. He also pulled me aside and caught me up on another killing.

Turns out the city of Fullerton had a bonafide serial killer. This would be the fifth body in as many months. He wanted me to come by the department tomorrow and compare notes, since I was an official consultant on the case. Sherbet was one of the few people who knew my super-secret identity. He and his wife stayed just long enough to drink some hot cider and eat some Christmas brownies, before moving on to another party.

Danny even stopped by to drop off the kids' presents. As he stood at the front door, peering over me into a home we had once shared together, no doubt taking in the dollar store decorations, the aromas, the laughter and even the corny Christmas music, he looked positively miserable and envious. I had it on good word that his relationship with his secretary was over. I also had it on good word that she was suing him for sexual harassment. Nice. But don't feel too bad for the guy. Apparently, he was now dating one of his strippers. Yes, my ex-husband, besides being an ambulance chaser, was also part-owner of a strip club in Colton.

Right. I couldn't be more proud.

As we stood awkwardly at the door, I sensed Kingsley watching us from within the living room, his hulking form backlit by the Christmas tree. Danny, it seemed, was waiting for an invitation to come in. This coming from a guy who was actively trying to ruin me. I thanked him for the presents, wished him a merry Christmas and, against my better judgment, gave him a half-hearted offer to come in, which he pounced on. He pushed past me and immediately went over to kitchen table where he began piling snacks on a paper plate.

Watching him, I reminded myself that it was Christmas, a day when even porn kings and slimeballs were given a one-day pardon.

When it came time for dinner, I thought of Fang alone in his little apartment. I had invited him, too, but was secretly relieved when he declined. He and Kingsley in the same room would have made everyone uncomfortable. Yes, Kingsley knew all about Fang. I believe in honesty and openness in a relationship. To a degree. Kingsley didn't need to know about Fang's criminal past.

I kept myself busy serving dinner, so busy that everyone forgot that I hadn't actually eaten. I would eat later tonight, with Kingsley. A rather nontraditional holiday meal, you could say.

With dinner over and dessert being served, I thought it best to step outside and get some fresh air. I excused myself, patting Kingsley's meaty thigh. He was deep in a conversation with, of all people, my ex-husband. Two attorneys talking shop.

Blech.

My house is small, but I have a big yard. I followed a curving, cement path that led from my front door to my garage, a path I had sprinted across many times during the heat of the day, each time gasping for breath and sometimes literally thinking I couldn't take another step. But I did it each and every day to pick up my kids from school.

A small price to pay.

The sun had long ago set. I felt strong and clear-headed. Cars were parked seemingly randomly outside my house. I lived in a narrow cul-de-sac, and parking here was always a challenge. Especially for Kingsley, who was a surprisingly bad parker. Even now, his black Escalade barely touching the curb, with most of the rear end blocking my driveway.

Pathetic. I expected more from an immortal with decades of driving experience.

I slipped my hands into my coat pocket and looked up into the evening sky. This would have been a good night for flying. Clear, cool skies, with Christmas tree lights sparkling far below. In fact, maybe I would try to get up tonight. Maybe fly out to see Kingsley later.

Maybe.

As I stepped out from behind the comically-parked Cadillac, I saw him standing there in the middle of the street, watching me.

Ishmael.

17.

Once again, I gasped.

"I didn't mean to startle you, Samantha."

"You have a way of doing that."

"Sometimes, I forget how easily humans startle. Humans...and vampires."

"I'm not human?"

"You haven't been human for many years, Sam."

"I feel human."

"Do you feel human when you're soaring above the earth?"

He stepped closer to me, hands clasped behind his back. To my eyes he seemed a little taller than I remembered.

He nodded. "I am taller, Sam. I am whatever

I choose to be."

Glowing particles of light swarmed around him...and disappeared into him. He was a being unlike anything I had ever seen. And to be clear, I've seen some weird shit.

But as he drew closer, walking casually with his hands behind his back, his movements so fluid and smooth that he appeared to be walking on air, I saw something else. Intermixed within the light particles were darker particles. The darker particles were new to me...and alarming. Never had I seen anything so black. Worse, the dark particles seemed to contaminate the light, spreading like a disease.

"A disease?" he said, nodding thoughtfully. "An interesting choice of words, since you yourself often call the darkness living within you a disease."

"There is no darkness in me."

Ishmael threw back his head and laughed, and it was the first time he had expressed real emotion. His first seeming loss of control. Everything prior to that, every move, every word, had seemed almost rehearsed.

"What do you think keeps you alive, Samantha Moon? What do you think you feed each and every time you consume blood? You're feeding the thing that lives within you."

"I am still me."

"Or so you think."

"I want you to leave."

He continued to approach me, continued his slow glide over the street tarmac. "You know so little, my dear. But I can show you so much. I can reveal it all to you. I can help you fight that which lives within you, that which is slowly consuming you."

Now he stood before me and, son of a bitch, he was even taller than just a few seconds before. By at least another six inches. Surely, he was taller now than even Kingsley.

I must be dreaming, I thought.

"You're not dreaming, Sam."

"Get the hell out of my head."

"I'm afraid I can't do that."

"Why?"

He reached out and touched me, running his fingers under my chin, lifting my face up to his. I shivered. His touch was hot. Almost superheated. "I don't want to get out of your head. Your thoughts are the only place I have sanctuary."

"I know what you are, and I'm telling you to leave me alone."

"Oh? And what am I, Sam?"

"A demon."

I could see the heartbreak in his eyes. He thought he could see me, but for the first time I was seeing him. He was lost, just as I felt lost sometimes. He had needs and desires, just as I did, and on this night, in the middle of this street, his eyes told me everything I needed to know. He was in love with me.

Could demons love? I didn't know, but I doubted it.

"Demon is such an ugly word, Sam."

"Then what are you?"

"I said it was ugly, I didn't say it was inaccurate."

I shuddered. The blackness swirled around him like black worms, weaving in and out of the light. "You look different."

"I am different. I gave up much to be with you, Sam."

"And you took much from me."

"I gave you immortality."

"You stole my humanity. You abused your power in the name of love. Or what you think of as love. You have put a curse on me that will never be fully released. You put me in danger and my own children in danger."

He laughed. "Your own immortality saved your boy from an agonizing death."

"If I had known that my immortality would be the only thing that would save my child, yes, I would have begged you to allow me to be attacked. To allow me to become what I am.

But you can't claim responsibility for a twist of fate."

Then again, maybe he could. I was in uncharted territory here. How much of the future did Ishmael know? Had he known that my son would acquire a terminal disease? I didn't know. Truth was, I didn't know what watchers were capable of and not capable of. But I knew something about free will, and I suspected Ishmael was pulling my strings like a puppet master. He was a person, a being, who had abused his influence.

"No," he said, reading my thoughts. "A person in love."

"You turned me into a monster," I said.

"Not a monster, Sam. An immortal. And the darkness that lives within you can be controlled. I can show you how. I can show you so many things."

"You *could* show me how? You *could* show me many things? Your love is conditional. Your love is not real. Whatever illusion you have about you and me ends tonight. You were given an amazing gift by the Almighty and you squandered it over illusions of love. You might have been able to read my thoughts, but you lacked something. Subtext. Hearing my thoughts isn't the same as experiencing my heart. Because if you ever had, you would have never done what you did to me on that night seven years ago."

"You have it all wrong, Sam. It was your destiny to become that which you are. I only helped...facilitate the process."

"I don't believe you."

"Believe what you will. But we are destined to be together, Samantha Moon. And when you are done playing with your dog, Kingsley, I will return for you."

And what happened next challenged my sanity. The solid man who had been standing before me, faded from view, and the particles of light that had been swarming around him winked out of existence, too.

I was left standing alone in the street.

18.

I was flying over Orange County.

The wind was cold, but my thick hide kept me comfortable. I was above a smattering of clouds, and far below, Christmas lights twinkled endlessly. From up here, it was very obvious that Californians were very much into the Christmas spirit.

I angled a little higher, caught a powerful jetstream, and was hurled along at a glorious rate. My thick, leathery wings were stretched taut, and a part of me wanted to just keep on flying, endlessly, to continuously trail behind the setting sun, to live in perpetual darkness forever.

A guardian angel had professed his love for

me. I suspected it was a misguided love. I suspected he was already well on his way to the dark side, that he had only used me to help facilitate the process. Whatever that process was.

And yet...

And yet, I felt his love for me. It had been real. I had seen it in his eyes, and heard it in his voice.

You can't fake love.

Or can you?

Yet, he could have gone about it a thousand different ways, a thousand better ways. Any of which would have gotten a better response from me.

We are destined to be together, he had said.

The San Gabriel Mountains appeared in the north, and I followed the contour of the ridge-line, rising and falling with the peaks and valleys, just a few feet above the pines and snow-covered cornices. Yes, even southern California gets snow, four thousand feet up.

I suspected that Ishmael had to break his connection to me, whatever that connection was. I suspected that, as my watcher, he was bound to me as my guardian.

But once I became immortal, all bets were off.

I angled up, followed a mountainous ridge,

and when the ridge dropped away, I kept angling up, flapping my wings harder and harder. Up I went, surging through vaporous clouds, blinded, until finally I broke through.

Above me was the half moon, shining brilliantly. I flew toward it, higher and higher, until ice crystals formed on my wings, until all oxygen disappeared in the air.

And there I hovered, briefly, at the far edges of our atmosphere, pondering destiny, until finally I tucked in my own wings and dove down, speeding through the night, faster than I had ever flown before...

After all, Christmas was over and I had a killer to find.

The End

Vampire Blues

One

On the way to Kingsley's, just as I passed under a massive billboard of Judge Judy smiling down warmly—yet judgmentally—my cell phone rang. I glanced at the faceplate. Caller unknown.

I clicked on my Bluetooth. "Moon Investigations."

"Hi," said the voice of an elderly lady. "I've never, you know, called a private investigator before. I'm a little nervous."

"We're just like other people," I said. "Just a lot cooler."

"Oh, ha-ha." She laughed good-naturedly. "Yes, I'm sure you are."

I headed up Bastanchury Avenue, which would soon loop me around to the foothills above Yorba Linda. "How can I help you?"

"Well, I need some help," she said, pausing. A pregnant pause. I knew pregnant pauses. She had a cheating husband on her hands.

"You think your husband's cheating on you," I said, gunning the minivan and just making it through a yellow light.

"How-how did you know?"

"Call it a hunch," I said. Actually, these days I didn't know what to call it. My old hunches and my powerful new sixth sense had fused into one. Hunch or not, I wasn't in the mood for another cheating spouse case. In fact, I could barely stomach them these days. I said, "I'm sorry to hear about your husband, but I'm a little booked right now. I know of a great detective out of Huntington Beach. Actually, don't let him know that I said that, since he's already got a big head—"

"No. Please. Please, I want a woman to help me. Only a woman." She took in a lot of air while I came to a stop at a red light. I was the only one sitting at the intersection. So, who was I waiting for? She went on, "I'm kind of down on men right now, if you know what I mean."

Actually, I did. I had gone through a similar reaction with my ex-husband, Danny. In fact, I even recalled writing to Fang that I hated all men.

I said, "I'm sure there are other female private investigators who would be more than happy—"

"There aren't. I've looked. You're the only one in the Yellow Pages. At least, the only one with a woman's name."

The light turned green. Kingsley was waiting for me with a chilled glass of the red stuff. I hadn't eaten in two days. I was ravenous and I was cranky. I said, "Let me be blunt: My own husband cheated on me not long ago. The very thought of working on another cheating spouse case turns my stomach. I'm just not the right person for this."

"I'm so sorry to hear that."

"Thank you," I said.

I could almost see her frowning. Hell, maybe I *could* see her frowning. In fact, the woman in my thoughts had a thick head of curly red hair. She looked a bit like Lucille Ball in her dotage. Then again, that could have all just been my imagination. And I'd always loved Lucille Ball.

"Well, thank you anyway," she said. "I will keep looking."

The pain in her voice found its way straight to my heart. Normally, such pain didn't register very deeply. After all, I spent half my time hearing heartbreaking stories. But this woman's pain reached me somehow. Perhaps because I had seen her in my thoughts. Or perhaps because she reminded me of Lucille Ball. Either way, I couldn't let her hang up just yet.

"Wait," I said. "Let me give you some advice. Ninety-five percent of the people who come to me with concerns of spousal misconduct are right."

"So, you're saying that more than likely he is cheating?"

"I'm saying that more than likely, your instincts are spot on."

In my mind, I could almost see her closing her eyes and nodding, her red, curly hair bouncing. "I see. Well, that's not good enough for me, Miss Moon. I need to know. I need to know for sure." There was a long pause and I could tell she was crying. "I won't trouble you any—"

"Wait," I said again, truly hating myself for what I was about to say next. I had a big case I was unofficially working with Detective Sherbet of the Fullerton P.D. and it was getting dangerous. I had stumbled across another victim of the "Orange County Stalker" that was only minutes old—the body still warm with blood pooling under the corpse. I had to stop myself from having a taste and leaving behind my DNA for the coroner's office. Self-discipline was a bitch, but far be it from me to taint a crime scene with my own genetic evidence. In the last hour, I had disentangled myself from giving my official statement to the FPD and a copy of my notes on the Orange County Stalker habits—I had worked up a decent profile on her. Yes, I said *her*. Sherbet was going to try to pay me for my work from some grant money for crime tippers which was way cool in my book since my kids both had dental appointments coming up. My sister, Mary Lou, had the kids at her house tonight and I planned to see Kingsley for some growly R&R and a much-needed feeding. I didn't have time for cheating spouses. I didn't want to deal with cheating spouses. I hated cheating spouses. But despite all of that, and my growling stomach, I heard myself say: "I'll help you. Tomorrow. The investigation on your husband should be a quick one."

She thanked me profusely, and when she was done, I asked why she thought her husband was cheating. As I wound my way to Kingsley's massive estate, she told me the usual story. Husband was staying out later than normal. Showering immediately when he came home. His excuses were never very good and she knew in her heart that he was lying. Her husband, apparently, had never been very good at lying.

Mostly, though, she was confused and lost. Her husband had been such a good man for so many years. A great provider. A great friend. Always there for her, even as she now battled cancer. Hell, even more so. Every day, he told her how much he loved her. Every day, he made her feel like a princess. She asked me why would he do this to her and I didn't have an answer, except to say that men were pigs. I immediately hated this one.

I gave her a checklist of information that I would need, including her hubby's personal and professional info and up to five recent pictures. I gave her my email address and she said she would get right on it. Whoopee.

She hung up, but before she did, she thanked me again. As I clicked off and pulled up to Kingsley's gaudy estate, I recognized the painful irony of the situation: She was thanking me to confirm her worst fears.

I had a helluva job.

Two

The next day, I had thirty minutes to kill before my appointment with Jacky, my boxing trainer.

Sitting in my minivan in the blessed shade of a pathetic magnolia tree, I went through my emails on the iPhone and found an attachment from one Gertrude Shine. The old lady from yesterday, I was sure of it. Sighing, I opened it and found five pictures of an aged man with a thick mustache. Included with the pictures was the man's personal information, and I was struck again by the intrusive nature of my job. The man in the photo was a complete stranger. But pretty soon, he would be all too familiar, so familiar that I would be instrumental in the destruction of his marriage.

No. *He* was instrumental in the destruction of the marriage. I was just reporting the facts.

I closed my eyes, rubbed them. I didn't have to take the job. I didn't have to take any job. Except Danny had yet to pony up any child support, let alone alimony, despite making five times what I made.

Despite openly cheating on me.

I studied the son of a bitch in the photos. Two of the photos depicted him standing with a large woman with red hair—the same woman, I wasn't too shocked to see, that I had seen in my thoughts.

I'm getting stronger, I thought. Indeed, my psychic powers now seemed to be increasing daily.

Anyway, the couple did not seem very happy, and I didn't think that was a psychic hit. Anyone looking at the pictures could see that. They weren't holding hands; in fact, they weren't really standing close to each other. The man was dumpy, but looked strong. Probably in his youth he had been an athlete but had let himself go to hell. He had broad shoulders that were mostly fat now. His mustache seemed to change from picture to picture, growing thicker and longer in some. I had asked for recent pictures, but these were clearly separated by months or even years.

I was parked on the street outside the gym, on a sweltering day in Southern California, where even in the shade the temperature was probably in the high eighties. I probably should have been sticky with sweat, but I wasn't. In fact, I was cold. So damn cold. Vampire cold.

Her husband's name was CS Shine, and according to Gertrude's email, that's all her husband went by: CS.

Seriously? What kind of pompous ass goes by initials these days? I never understood it and probably never would. Initials did not a name make.

CS Shine. He sounded like a cruise ship.

Anyway, CS *Dumbass* actually worked nearby—at a bakery of all places.

So, I checked the time on my cell, saw that I had another twenty-five minutes before Jacky would start yelling at me to keep my boxing hands up, then started the minivan and headed east on Commonwealth.

To the only bakery in town.

And to CS Dipshit.

Three

I'd seen the bakery over the years, but had never made it inside. And since I doubted they served plasma-filled turnovers, these days, I had even less reason to go inside.

For now, though, I parked across the street and took in the scene. We were still technically in downtown Fullerton, but we were pushing it. The buildings here were mostly part of newer chains, with hipster apartments above and clean sidewalks out front. Part of Fullerton's attempt to commercialize its downtown. For the most part, the idea worked. The older stores had gotten a facelift, and now the whole area was buzzing with activity.

The bakery had a decidedly Old World feel to it, as if it had been transplanted brick by brick from the back streets of Italy or France. It was tucked between some of the newer buildings, and I could just see the owner, CS Loser, indignantly holding his ground, progress be damned. No doubt, he had turned down large of sums of money to buy his bakery, thumbing his nose at the establishment.

Of course, I could be wrong, but this was a borderline psychic hit. If so, you could take it to the bank.

Anyway, the windows out front advertised cream puffs and fresh baked breads. There was a yellowed poster of an apple pie in the window. Another displayed a stack of what had once been a fresh-baked batch of cookies. Now they were so faded they could have been a pile of cow pies.

Undeterred by the shabby window dressings, customers poured in and out of the bakery. Many held pink boxes or white bags. I was willing to bet that Detective Sherbet of the Fullerton P.D. frequented the place. Stereotypical, I knew, but the man had a huge sweet tooth. He also had a nice, round belly. The two were not mutually exclusive.

Through the dusty glass, I could see a man working. An older man wearing an apron. There was also a much younger woman working there, too. A cute younger woman who smiled a lot through the window, and it was obvious that she made every customer feel welcome. I hated her immediately. Home-wrecking bitch.

Easy, girl. You don't know that.

Girls who smiled at everyone made me nervous. Married men responded to those smiles. Married men thought those smiles were directed only at them. Married men acted on those smiles in stupid ways.

Especially married bosses.

I watched the scene for the next twenty minutes, absorbing the details of the girl, of the man, the way they seemed to work effortlessly in tandem. Sometimes, he appeared out front and graciously spoke to customers. Mostly, he worked in the back, no doubt making his pies and cakes and all the things that I couldn't touch with a ten-foot pole.

By the time I left, I was certain the two were a little too chummy, a little too comfortable. Something was up. That much was certain, and Gertrude, I think, had every right to be suspicious.

Now, she just needed proof, and that was the hard part.

Four

Mary Lou and I had just finished our weekly round of drinks at Hero's. Yes, I still frequented Hero's. Yes, I still IM'd Fang. Yes, I knew he was a killer.

Aaron Parker, aka Fang, raised serious moral issues with me, moral issues that I often struggled with. That he was a head case, there was no doubt. Anyone who grew up in the environment in which he had grown up, in the circumstances in which he had grown up, would have had similar issues. Or not. Perhaps it was a perfect storm of craziness and circumstance.

Either way, at age seventeen, a very delusional Aaron Parker had killed his girlfriend, sucking her dry. His story had been a sensational one. Even more sensational was that the young man had escaped a high-security psychiatry ward, killing two more men in the process.

That had been almost two decades ago. Aaron Parker, of course, now went by an assumed name, and as far as I could tell, he had had some facial reconstruction surgery. He was still a wanted man, and he just so happened to be our bartender and my confidant.

No, I hadn't known about his past. I didn't know who the hell he was, truth be known, until six months ago, when we had met for the first time. Or, rather, when he had re-introduced himself. Turned out that he had stalked me and found out who I was and where I lived.

And this was where I struggled. Fang had proven time and again, to have my best interests at heart. That he was obsessed with vampires was another thing entirely. Another thing that I chose to ignore. In fact, I chose to see only his good side, a side that had been touching and human and endlessly informative.

Therein lay my quandary.

I had grown close to him over the years—very close. It wasn't until six years had passed that the truth came out. I should have been pissed. I should have felt violated. To be sure, I had flirted with both emotions. Mostly, in the end, I saw him as a deeply troubled man.

Not to mention, we had a psychic connection that I couldn't quite place my finger on. No doubt the connection was rooted in our close friendship. Indeed, the closer I got to people, the more I could read their minds. The interesting thing about Fang was this: he could also read my mind.

I hadn't been ready for that.

He liked to remind me that we were both flawed. That we had both killed. That we were both victims of circumstance. He liked to remind me that he had never intended to kill his girlfriend. It had been an accident. Two people had gone too far in the throes of lovemaking. And one of them had ended up dead.

Yes, Fang and I were friends. Yes, he had wanted much more, but I had questioned his motives. It seemed to me that he loved me for my gifts. Like a star-crossed fan. I questioned his motives, especially when he asked me to turn him into a vampire.

No, I hadn't turned him, but we remained friends, even while I continued to date Kingsley.

So, when we left the bar on this quiet evening, with Fang and I having made small talk both audibly and inaudibly, I saw something that surprised the hell out of me. Something made me turn back and pause, and as I did so, I spotted CS Dipstick working his way through the bar. I stood there with my sister and tried not to stare as the older baker worked his way out of the bar, passed us, and headed outside. A strong plume of vaporous alcohol trailed behind him.

The man certainly didn't look like an adulterer. He looked tired, worn down, and at his wits' end.

Maybe because of all the extramarital sex, I thought. The thought really didn't stick. Frowning after him, I excused myself from my sister and followed him out.

Five

CS Numbnuts was walking down a fairly busy sidewalk.

I trailed behind him a dozen feet, keeping my head down and my hands in my pockets. I passed a half dozen well-dressed couples, ranging from old to young. Some of the younger couples veered off into Hero's. I slid behind an older couple who were laughing and walking while holding hands. Little did they know they were being used as my cover. Or that an honest-to-God vampire was just steps behind them.

If so, I doubted the woman would have nonchalantly reached down and squeezed the older guy's buns. Or what passed as buns, since there was nothing really there. Still, he laughed uproariously, and I was beginning to suspect that someone was going to pop a little blue pill tonight.

The older couple moved at a much slower pace than I would have liked, especially now that the woman had found her man's non-ass, and as they strolled and squeezed and laughed, the baker made a right turn through some buildings and disappeared into the shadows.

Shadows weren't a problem for me. Hell, I specialized in shadows. With my target out of sight, I quickly slipped past the horny old couple. But before I did, I squeezed the man's ass to see what the fuss was all about. At least I think I squeezed it. I might have hit all bone. Either way, he yelped and jumped about two feet and the woman shot me a furious look.

"Sorry," I said, speaking over my shoulder. "I thought you were someone else."

Although technically a parking lot, this was really nothing more than a glorified alley, overflow for the bar. At the far end, a pair of brake lights flashed. I ducked between two cars and crouched, watching as a beat-up van backed out slowly and carefully. I caught the profile of the baker as he worked the gear shift in the darkened alley. His profile came sharply into view, alight with the glowing particles that someone like me could somehow see. He was an old, tired man. Too tired for an affair, if you asked me.

So, what the hell was going on?

Shortly, he must have found the drive gear, because now he was rolling forward and quickly picking up speed, moving opposite me to the far end of the alley. I briefly debated what to do, since he was now heading in the opposite direction of my parked minivan, which was in the bar's main parking lot a half block away.

I could run to my minivan, but I risked losing him.

Or I could run after him...and risk looking like a freak.

I thought about this, chewing my lower lip, and as he reached the far end of the alley—and actually turned on his blinker—I made a decision.

As he hung a right and headed up Amerige Street, I dashed after him.

Let the freak show begin...

Six

I quickly covered the space between the alley and the street.

I slowed when I came up to Amerige Street. I rarely spoke of or utilized this particular talent, one that I had discovered years ago: the ability to move *fast*. I had the ability to cover ground so quickly that at times, I thought I was flying.

I mean, how often did one need to dash down a street? I wasn't a superhero. I wasn't a cop. I didn't chase down bad guys. And I wasn't in an Adam Sandler movie, where I would use my speed to win track races and collect babes. It was just something I could do, something I could tap into when needed.

And tonight, caught between an alley and

blocks away from my minivan—and not knowing where CS Adulterer was headed—well, I had little other choice.

I was wearing my Nike running shoes, a cute pair with a yellow swoosh that matched the yellow ribbon in my hair. I doubted the Nike designers ever conducted a field test like this before.

Amerige is a quiet street that runs north and south, paralleling Harbor Boulevard, itself running through the heart of downtown Fullerton.

A car was coming from my left, and there was a couple walking toward me a half block down. I ducked my head and hung a right, spying the van's taillights in the far distance. CS Asshole was easily three blocks ahead of me, having clearly caught a few green lights.

I jogged at first, my legs feeling strong and mechanical, two pistons attached to a five-foot, three-inch frame. I stepped off the sidewalk and jogged along the street next to a row of parked cars. I picked up speed gradually, keeping the van in sight.

The couple whipped past me, a blur, really. I saw the man's head snap around, following. Or trying to follow me. No doubt his jaw had dropped open, too.

I chuckled and lowered my shoulders,

picking up speed. Street signs, small trees, and fire hydrants all whipped past me. A small dog barked at me from an open car window, but its yipping receded behind me almost instantly.

I came to the first intersection, and I was in luck. A green light. I debated slowing. The debate didn't last long when I spied the van hang a left far ahead.

I hit another gear entirely. A gear I didn't know I had.

Lights blurred past me so fast that I shouldn't have been able to control my body. I should have been completely out of control, slamming into whatever crossed paths in front of me. But it was the opposite. I had *complete control* of my body—and I saw everything with clarity. Perhaps even supernatural clarity, nearly predicting where cars and people would be.

Wind thundered over me, plastering my clothing to my skin, whipping my hair into a crazed frenzy.

My legs felt so damn strong. My energy endless.

I could do this all night. All the way to the rising sun.

I'm not sure what people saw, or what they think they saw, or even if they actually did see me. I was through the intersection so fast that if someone looked down, or looked away, or even blinked, they would have missed me.

I felt movement to my right and veered away just as a car pulled rapidly away from the curb and hung a U-turn. The driver never saw me, I was sure of it.

The light at the next intersection was red. I slowed down gradually, reluctantly, coming up behind a row of cars. I sidestepped smoothly onto the sidewalk and wove quickly through a group of women who were much too loud and drunk. I suspected I was in the midst of one of those "girls' nights out" that I'm always hearing about. Did drinking with my sister count?

By the time I reached the sidewalk, the light had turned green. I crossed with the others, except, unlike the others, I was already on the far side of the street before they had taken a few steps. I heard gasps behind me, and saw many heads turn, but they were now so far behind me that I didn't care and I'm sure they were doubting their own sanity.

And now I was running so fast that I wasn't entirely certain that my feet were touching the ground. Wind blasted me. Lights streaked. Bugs were obliterated.

The next light was green and I was just a blur. I felt like a blur, too. I felt inhuman. I felt elemental. Like the wind. Something from the sky, the earth.

Cars came and went. People came and went. I swerved, I dodged, I hauled ass, and finally, I hung a left and was nearly upon the van, which was just turning into a warehouse.

I swerved to the other side of the street and spent a few seconds coming to a full stop. I might be immortal, but I still had to contend with physics. Well, sort of. Cars are manufactured with brakes. Bi-peds? Not so much.

From behind an old-school station wagon, I watched the van come to a complete stop along the side of the building. The baker emerged from the van, and as he did so, a car door opened from another vehicle parked near the warehouse.

His pretty young assistant stepped out and met him with a warm hug. *Bingo!*

Together they slipped inside the dark building through a side door. My mind raced. What was this place? What the hell was going on? I didn't know the answers to either question, but one thing I did know: Men were fucking pigs.

Seven

I stepped up to the building and scanned it.

So what kind of building was this? Why were they here after hours? Was this some kind of underground sex club? Were unspeakable sexual acts being performed just behind these doors? I pictured a sea of naked bodies, all undulating rhythmically to hypnotic music, drugs everywhere, naked limbs everywhere, penises and breasts and sex toys galore.

But I knew this wasn't right. This was just my imagination running wild. Far different than a psychic hit.

Still, I listened for music, for the thumping of bass, for *anything*, but heard nothing other than a faint, echoing hammering sound which could have come from anywhere.

No. Wait. Laughter. Yes, I just heard laughter coming from within the building.

The bastard. He had no business laughing with another woman, not with a dying wife waiting for him at home.

The bastard.

I stepped back and scanned the facade. Nothing to indicate what the building was. I had a thought and removed my iPhone. I Google-mapped the area and a moment later, the same city street popped up on my screen. This time in bright daylight.

Ah, there we go. According to Google Maps, the area was known as Al's Auto. I pocketed the phone and did some frowning.

Al's Auto? What the hell?

I didn't know what was going on, but I knew one thing: a married man had met his cute assistant in an apparent abandoned building late at night, leaving his sick wife to die alone.

Yeah, men are fucking pigs.

Of course, I was a little biased these days.

Keeping to the shadows of a pathetic tree rising up from a trash-strewn sidewalk planter, I closed my eyes and utilized some of my newfound skills, clearing my mind and doing my best to remove some of the burning hate that I was feeling for the cheating bastard. With eyes closed, I expanded my awareness. I imagined this as a glowing arc, widening around me like ripples in a pond. The glowing arc was my feelers, my tentacles, my supernatural eyes and ears and hands and feet. It kept widening. I sensed a nearby mailbox. There was a rat watching me from a drain grate. Correction, *three* rats, all with glowing eyes, attracted to me for reasons I couldn't quite understand. There was also an orange tabby that had made its way from the alley to sit under the baker's van. The tabby was watching the rats, its tail swooshing spasmodically. I could almost—almost—hear the growling of its stomach. Maybe I sensed its hunger. Anyway, the arc continued out, widening, now reaching its curious supernatural feelers deep into the Al's Auto. I saw a simple front office. Two simple front offices, actually. Computers. Desks. Filing cabinets. Pictures of sports cars on the walls. The building wasn't abandoned. It was perfectly functioning. I sensed a hallway that led into the back of the shop. I pushed through a doorway into a brightly lit room. Lots of images here. Murky images. Clear images. Cars lined up. Cars on lifts. Another bigger image under what appeared to be a tarp. But I was reaching the end of my range. The images were getting murkier, fuzzier, more scattered. I was certain there was a man lying on the ground.

Correction: *two* men lying on the ground. Or perhaps kneeling; it was hard to tell. Were they dead? Again, impossible to tell. And now, I saw something else. Or *someone* else. A woman was squatting over one of them. The images were distorted at best. What they were doing exactly was impossible to tell. What I inferred they were doing was another story.

My consciousness snapped back to the street, stunned.

I opened my eyes and, briefly confused, got my bearings. A scratching sound came from my right. I turned and saw the bright eyes of one of the rats. Watching me. He had inched a little closer.

I ignored the rat and did the only thing I could think of. My client wanted evidence. I would give her evidence. I didn't have time to mess around with this case. I had other, more important cases. Bigger cases.

One and done, I thought. It was time to end this case.

I pulled out my iPhone once again, but this time, I called Mrs. Shine.

Eight

We were in the alleyway.

Gertrude Shine was a heavy-set woman with swollen ankles, so swollen that the hem of her stretch pants were stretched to the limit. Her hair was indeed red and permed, and she was the spitting image of the woman I had seen in my thoughts.

Anyway, I felt horrible for bringing her out here, especially in her current condition, but people didn't pay me to tell them good news. They already knew, in their hearts, that bad news was coming. I was simply a facilitator of bad news, which was a shitty way of looking at my job. Or an aspect of my job, but there you have it. Had I more time, I would have waited around and tried to photograph the adoring couple as they left the building, ideally hand-in-hand, and no doubt, with a long kiss goodbye. People generally didn't hump in public, and, by law, I couldn't photograph through windows. Major invasion of privacy. So, catching a couple on a date, kissing in public, and generally acting lovie-dovie was the best any private eye can hope for. And it was generally enough for most people.

Well, screw all that.

The woman was dying. Her husband was a snake, and I had bigger fish to fry.

"He's in there?" asked Gertrude. She seemed to be having problems standing and she was definitely having problems breathing. I was worried for her, but she didn't complain.

I nodded, and she set her jaw determinedly.

"With her?"

"And one other," I said.

"Who?"

"I don't know."

"I'm confused," she said.

"So am I," I said.

Minutes earlier she had parked across the street, and I had led her back here to the alley behind the auto shop. Before us were two massive fold-up doors, so big they could have housed a dirigible. Lights flickered beyond the dirty windows. I heard voices, laughter. As far as I was aware, only three people were inside.

The back alley was similar in layout to Hero's; meaning, the space behind the shop was also a small parking lot that bled into a much darker alley. If I hadn't been so tough, I might have looked nervously down the alleys.

I was, and I didn't.

The air was heavy and still. Mrs. Shine was sweating profusely and waving her hand in front of her face. It was time to get on with it.

"So, you have no idea who owns this building?" I asked.

"None."

I went over to the first of the garage doors and studied it. Two big padlocks. I reached down and gripped the handle.

"But isn't it locked?" asked Gertrude, stepping behind me.

I was feeling sassy and impatient and even small lies seemed a waste of time.

"Not anymore," I said, and yanked hard on the handle. Both locks held tight, but I couldn't say the same for the latches. They ripped apart and tumbled to the cracked concrete, even while I continued pulling up the rolling door.

Light spilled out.

Blinding light.

Behind me, Mrs. Shine gasped. I didn't gasp, but my jaw did drop open.

Nine

Three people jumped in unison.

One of the guys who jumped was unfortunately working under what appeared to be a massive propeller. As he leaped, he slammed his head hard, instantly opening a gash along his hairline. Blood poured freely from his skull and he cursed. Before I could stop myself, I licked my lips.

"Jesus H. Christ!" he shouted, holding his head.

We seemed to have caught the young woman, who had been kneeling next to him, in the act of handing him a tool. Holding a wrench, she gasped and spun around. She was, of course, the baker's assistant. Apparently, she was also a mechanic's assistant, too.

The baker himself had been lying on a tarp and painting the hull of what I could see now was a good-sized boat. In his alarm, he had kicked over the can of paint which spilled across the tarp and over onto the oil-stained cement floor.

The young guy holding his bleeding head marched over to us, holding his wrench rather threateningly. I was still stunned, still soaking in the scene, still realizing I had made an egregious error.

So had Gertrude Shine.

The young man with the wrench said, "What the hell's going on here?"

Blood had found its way between his fingers. I was too alarmed to pay much attention to it. Well, not too much. I did notice how the overhead lights reflected dully off it. Perfectly off it. He was looking around wildly, trying, no doubt, to figure out how we had gotten in. He walked briefly outside and saw his destroyed garage door.

"What the fuck?"

I said nothing. There was nothing to say. Something like this could cost me my private investigator's license. I hadn't been thinking. I hadn't been thinking for a few days now. Hell, even longer. After all, Orange County was being stalked by a sick son-of-a-bitch, and I had found myself in the thick of it.

But I couldn't think about that now.

I blinked. Coming back to my senses. What had I done? Sure, I might have talked my way out of something like this, but it was impossible with Gertrude next to me. Her husband, CS Shine, came over to her, equally stunned. There was a big blotch of cream-colored paint on his hip where the pail had been knocked over and washed over him.

"Trudy?" he said, looking from her, to me, to the broken door, to his bleeding mechanic friend. "Trudy, what's going on?"

I looked at her and saw that she was crying, holding her hands over her face. She was looking up at the stern, the back of the boat where the massive propeller was mounted. Although most of the boat was covered in a blue tarp, the stern was exposed, perhaps so the mechanic could have a go at the engine. Painted in fancy black script above the propeller were the words "Gertrude Forever."

"I don't understand," she said, but she was crying, so of course she understood. Perfectly.

He smiled at her patiently, and I saw the love radiating from him. Literally. I could see the warm, violet waves emanating from the light field that surrounded him, reaching out to her. "You always wanted to travel the world, honey, and now we can. We've been overhauling it. Al, Becky's boyfriend, has been letting me use his shop and helping me rebuild the engine."

She buried her face in her hands. "I thought you were..." But she couldn't finish her words.

"Having an affair?"

He smiled warmly, and instead of defending himself or laughing off her insecurity, Mr. CS Shine went over to his wife and gave her a big, smothering hug, and I heard the intimate words he whispered softly into her ear, "Ah, my sweetheart. Don't you know by now you're my precious girl?"

"I'm so sorry—"

But he shushed her and held her, and his words hit me hard. I fought my own tears and mostly won.

Just then, the young mechanic appeared in front of me. "Someone's paying for my door and for this." He pointed to the gash in his forehead.

I told him I would. I told him I would do anything he needed. I gave him my card and he nodded, and I could see the questioning look in his eyes, even though he didn't voice his thoughts:

How the hell had we broken his door?

But I only smiled weakly at him, told him to

send me any bills. Mr. and Mrs. Shine were pressed tightly in each other's arms and the mechanic bled into a dew rag pressed tightly to his head.

Okay, I conceded. *Some* men weren't assholes.

Some men were *angels*.

I slipped away from the embracing couple. Into the night. Where I belonged.

The End

About the Author:

J.R. Rain is an ex-private investigator who now writes full-time. He lives in a small house on a small island with his small dog, Sadie. Please visit him at www.jrrain.com.

Made in the USA
Monee, IL
27 February 2020